봄·봄

아시아에서는 《바이링궐 에디션 한국 대표 소설》을 기획하여 한국의 우수한 문학을 주제별로 엄선해 국내외 독자들에게 소개합니다. 이 기획은 국내외 우수한 번역가들이 참여하여 원작의 품격을 최대한 살렸습니다. 문학을 통해 아시아의 정체성과 가치를 살피는 데 주력해 온 아시아는 한국인의 삶을 넓고 깊게 이해하는 데 이 기획이 기여하기를 기대합니다.

Asia Publishers presents some of the very best modern Korean literature to readers worldwide through its new Korean literature series 〈Bilingual Edition Modern Korean Literature〉. We are proud and happy to offer it in the most authoritative translation by renowned translators of Korean literature. We hope that this series helps to build solid bridges between citizens of the world and Koreans through a rich in-depth understanding of Korea.

바이링궐 에디션 한국 대표 소설 096

Bi-lingual Edition Modern Korean Literature 096

# Spring, Spring

# 김유정

## 봄 · 봄

# Kim Yu-jeong

ASIA
PUBLISHERS

Contents

봄 · 봄                          007
Spring, Spring


해설                            059
Afterword


비평의 목소리                     071
Critical Acclaim


작가 소개                        076
About the Author

# 봄·봄

Spring, Spring

"장인님! 인젠 저……."

내가 이렇게 뒤통수를 긁고, 나이가 찼으니 성례를 시켜 줘야 하지 않겠느냐고 하면 대답이 늘,

"이 자식아! 성례구 뭐구 미처 자라야지!"

하고 만다.

이 자라야 한다는 것은 내가 아니라 장차 내 아내가 될 점순이의 키 말이다.

내가 여기에 와서 돈 한 푼 안 받고 일하기를 삼 년하고 꼬박이 일곱 달 동안을 했다. 그런데도 미처 못 자랐다니까 이 키는 언제야 자라는 겐지 짜장[1] 영문 모른다. 일을 좀 더 잘해야 한다든지 혹은 밥을 (많이 먹는다고 노

"Father-in-law, sir! Please, do you think now it's about the time...?"

When I scratch the back of my head and ask my father-in-law to allow us to marry—as she's old enough now—the answer is, without fail, "You, fool! Still gotta grow up a little more if you want have your wedding!" The person he's talking about who has to grow up isn't me, actually. It's Jeom-sun, my bride-to-be.

I've worked at his house for free for no less than three years and seven months. Still he claims that she's not grown enough yet, so I really have no idea when she's gonna be the right size. If he says

9

상 걱정이니까) 좀 덜 먹어야 한다든지 하면 나도 얼마든지 할 말이 많다. 하지만 점순이가 아직 어리니까 더 자라야 한다는 여기에는 어째 볼 수 없이 그만 병병하고[2] 만다.

이래서 나는 애최 계약이 잘못된 걸 알았다. 이태면 이태, 삼 년이면 삼 년, 기한을 딱 작정하고 일을 했어야 원 할 것이다. 덮어놓고 딸이 자라는 대로 성례를 시켜 주마, 했으니 누가 늘 지키고 섰는 것도 아니고 그 키가 언제 자라는지 알 수 있는가. 그리고 난 사람의 키가 무럭무럭 자라는 줄만 알았지 붙박이 키에 모로만 벌어지는 몸도 있는 것을 누가 알았으랴. 때가 되면 장인님이 어련하랴 싶어서 군소리 없이 꾸벅꾸벅 일만 해왔다. 그럼 말이다, 장인님이 제가 다 알아차려서,

"어 참, 너 일 많이 했다. 고만 장가들어라."

하고 살림도 내주고 해야 나도 좋을 것이 아니냐. 시치미를 딱 떼고 도리어 그런 소리가 나올까 봐서 지레 펄펄 뛰고 이 야단이다. 명색이 좋아 데릴사위지 일하기에 싱겁기도 할 뿐더러 이건 참 아무것도 아니다.

숙맥이 그걸 모르고 점순이의 키 자라기만 까맣게 기다리지 않았나.

that I need to work harder or maybe I should eat less (since he complains about my eating too much all the time), I've got a lot to say. But, when he says that Jeom-sun is still too young and she's gotta grow up more, then I really feel at a loss; I just don't know what to do.

So I realize that this contract was flawed from the beginning. I should have made an agreement about the set period, two, or three years, before I began to work for him. He'd just mentioned giving us a wedding when his daughter was of age, but how was I supposed to know when that would happen unless I kept an eye on her all the time? And, since I thought people only grew taller, how was I supposed to know there were people whose bodies only grew sideways? I trusted that my father-in-law would take care of us when the time came, and so I just worked obediently without complaint. So, then, shouldn't he appreciate me a little more and say, "Oh, wow, you have worked so much. Now, looks like it's time for that wedding of yours!" and then, offer to set us up in a separate family? I'd be happy then, right? Instead, he plays innocent and makes a big fuss if I should say something like that. I'm his live-in son-in-law in name only, and I don't

언젠가는 하도 갑갑해서 자를 가지고 덤벼들어서 그 키를 한번 재볼까 했다마는, 우리는 장인님이 내외를 해야 한다고 해서 마주 서 이야기도 한마디 하는 법 없다. 우물길에서 어쩌다 마주칠 적이면 겨우 눈어림으로 재보고 하는 것인데 그럴 적마다 나는 저만큼 가서,

"제—미 키두!"

하고 논둑에다 침을 퉤, 뱉는다. 아무리 잘 봐야 내 겨드랑(다른 사람보다 좀 크긴 하지만) 밑에서 넘을락 말락 밤낮요 모양이다. 개돼지는 푹푹 크는데 왜 이리도 사람은 안 크는지, 한동안 머리가 아프도록 궁리도 해보았다. 아하, 물동이를 자꾸 이니까 뼈다귀가 움츠러드나 보다, 하고 내가 넌짓넌짓이 그 물을 대신 길어도 주었다. 뿐만 아니라 나무를 하러 가면 서낭당에 돌을 올려놓고,

"점순이의 키 좀 크게 해줍소사. 그러면 담엔 떡 갖다 놓고 고사드립죠니까."

하고 치성도 한두 번 드린 것이 아니다. 어떻게 돼먹은 킨지 이래도 막무가내니……

그래 내 어저께 싸운 것이지 결코 장인님이 밉다든가 해서가 아니다.

feel like keeping up this work senselessly. Point-less. That's what I feel like this has become.

How stupid I've been! Just waiting and waiting forever for Jeom-sun to get a little bigger!

One day, I felt so frustrated that I tried to measure her height with a ruler myself. But, Father-in-law said that we should avoid the opposite sex—manners and all—so we can't even stand face to face to chat. Whenever I run into her on our way to and from the well, I try to size her up by eye. Every time, I walk a few paces, I spit on a ridge between the rice fields, and I say, "Shit, what a size!"

No matter how favorably I try to size her up, she always only comes up to about my armpit (though I'm a bit taller than most other people)—that's just how big she is. While dogs and pigs are growing, and growing quickly, why can't people grow this way? I wracked my brain about it for a while. I thought, Aha, her bones must be shrinking because she carries a water jar on her head all the time! I've secretly carried water for her before she did. Also, whenever I went to gather firewood, I offered a rock to the shrine of a tutelary deity and pray over and over again, "Please grow Jeom-sun taller...next time I'll offer rice cakes..." Still, that good-for-nothing

모를 붓다가[3] 가만히 생각을 해보니까 또 싱겁다. 이 벼가 자라서 점순이가 먹고 좀 큰다면 모르지만 그렇지도 못한 걸 내 심어서 뭘 하는 거냐. 해마다 앞으로 축 거불지는[4] 장인님의 아랫배(가 너무 먹은 걸 모르고 내병[5]이라나, 그 배)를 불리기 위하여 심곤 조금도 싶지 않다.

"아이구 배야!"

난 물 붓다 말고 배를 쓰다듬으면서 그대로 논둑으로 기어올랐다. 그리고 겨드랑에 꼈던 벼 담긴 키를 그냥 땅바닥에 털썩, 떨어치며 나도 털썩 주저앉았다. 일이 암만 바빠도 나 배 아프면 고만이니까. 아픈 사람이 누가 일을 하느냐. 파릇파릇 돋아 오른 풀 한 숲[6]을 뜯어 들고 다리의 거머리를 쓱쓱 문대며 장인님의 얼굴을 쳐다보았다.

논 가운데서 장인님이 이상한 눈을 해 가지고 한참을 날 노려보더니,

"너 이 자식, 왜 또 이래 응?"

"배가 좀 아파서유!"

하고 풀 위에 슬며시 쓰러지니까 장인님은 약이 올랐다. 저도 논에서 철벙철벙 둑으로 올라오더니 잡은 참 내 멱살을 움켜잡고 뺨을 치는 것이 아닌가.

height of hers stays the same...

That's why I argued with Father-in-law, not because I hate him or anything.

I was transplanting rice seedlings, and I thought about the situation again and I couldn't help feeling like it was pointless. What was the point of my planting rice seedlings unless Jeom-sun would grow up on the rice grown out of them? I didn't want to plant them to fill Father-in-law's ever-bulging belly (Never realizes he's overeating. Says that's because of his stomach trouble. Huh, that belly!)

"Oh my stomach!"

In the middle of moving the rice seedlings, I rub my belly and clamber over a ridge between the rice fields. Then, dropping the winnowing basket I had under my arm, I sat down plump. 'Cause no matter how busy the work is, you can't do a thing if you got a stomachache. How can a sick person work? I pulled a handful of green grass and rubbed it on my leg to rid myself of a leech, watching Father-in-law's face.

Father-in-law glared at me for a while from the middle of a rice paddy. Then he said: "You, little... what's the matter with you again, huh?"

"Got a stomachache!"

"이 자식아, 일허다 말면 누굴 망해 놀 셈속이냐. 이 대가릴 까놀 자식!"

우리 장인님은 약이 오르면 이렇게 손버릇이 아주 못 됐다. 또 사위에게 이 자식 저 자식 하는 이놈의 장인님은 어디 있느냐. 오죽해야 우리 동리에서 누굴 물론하고 그에게 욕을 안 먹는 사람은 명이 짧다 한다. 조그만 아이들까지도 그를 돌아 세 놓고[7] 욕필이(본 이름이 봉필이니까), 욕필이, 하고 손가락질을 할 만치 두루 인심을 잃었다. 허나 인심을 정말 잃었다면 욕보다 읍의 배 참봉댁 마름[8]으로 더 잃었다. 번히 마름이란 욕 잘하고 사람 잘 치고 그리고 생김 생기길 호박개[9] 같아야 쓰는 거지만 장인님은 외양이 똑 됐다. 작인[10]이 닭 마리나 좀 보내지 않는다든가 애벌논[11]때 품을 좀 안 준다든가 하면 그해 가을에는 영락없이 땅이 뚝뚝 떨어진다. 그러면 미리부터 돈도 먹이고 술도 먹이고 안달재신[12]으로 돌아치던 놈이 그 땅을 슬쩍 돌라안는다.[13] 이 바람에 장인님 집 빈 외양간에는 눈깔 커다란 황소 한 놈이 절로 엉금엉금 기어들고, 동리 사람들은 그 욕을 다 먹어 가면서도 그래도 굽신굽신하는 게 아닌가.

그러나 내겐 장인님이 감히 큰소리할 계제가 못 된다.

Then, I lay down on the grass, which irritated Father-in-law. Why, he went splashing through the rice paddy all the way to the ridge, grabbed me by the collar, and slapped me across my face!

"You, son-of-a-bitch! So, you gonna stop working and try to ruin me? You deserve a knock to the head!"

When you get him angry, Father-in-law can have some very loose fists. Also, what kind of father-in-law calls his own son-in-law names? He's so foul-mouthed that villagers say that anyone who hasn't been called names by him won't live long.[1] He's lost the hearts of so many villagers that even the littlest children call him Foul-mouth-pil—his name is Bong-pil—behind his back. Speaking of losing villagers' hearts, more than his habit of calling people names, he really lost the love of the villagers with his work as the supervisor of Chambong Bae's tenant farms.[2] It's usually expected for a supervisor of a tenant farm to be foul-mouthed and violent, to look like a stoutly built, hairy dog. But Father-in-law really fit the bill. If a tenant farmer didn't occasionally send a chicken or two, or offer free labor during the initial weeding season, he was sure to lose his farm under Father-in-law's supervision that

17

뒷생각은 못 하고 뺨 한 개를 딱 때려놓고는 장인님은 무색해서 덤덤히 쓴침만 삼킨다. 난 그 속을 퍽 잘 안다. 조금 있으면 갈[14]도 꺾어야 하고 모도 내야 하고, 한창 바쁜 때인데 나 일 안 하고 우리 집으로 그냥 가면 고만이니까. 작년 이맘때도 트집을 좀 하니까 늦잠 잔다고 돌멩이를 집어 던져서 자는 놈의 발목을 삐게 해놨다. 사날씩이나 건성 끙끙 앓았더니 종당에는 거반 울상이 되지 않았는가.

"얘, 그만 일어나 일 좀 해라. 그래야 올 갈에 벼 잘되면 너 장가들지 않니?"

그래 귀가 번쩍 뜨여서 그날로 일어나서 남이 이틀 품 들일 논을 혼자 삶아[15] 놓으니까 장인님도 눈깔이 커다랗게 놀랐다. 그럼 정말로 가을에 와서 혼인을 시켜 줘야 온 경위가 옳지 않겠나. 볏섬을 척척 들여 쌓아도 다른 소리는 없고 물동이를 이고 들어오는 점순이를 담배통으로 가리키며,

"이 자식아, 미처 커야지. 조걸 데리구 무슨 혼인을 한다구 그러니 온!"

하고 남 낯짝만 붉게 해주고 고만이다. 골김[16]에 그저 이놈의 장인님, 하고 댓돌에다 메꽂고 우리 고향으로

18

fall. Then, someone, who has been anxiously bribing him with money and wine, would snatch the farm up from right under their noses. That's why a wide-eyed ox crawled freely into Father-in-law's empty stable and villagers kowtowed before him despite all his name-calling!

Nevertheless, Father-in-law could not afford to yell at me.

After thoughtlessly slapping me on the cheek, he had to swallow his own bitter saliva silently. I knew very well what was going through his mind then. A very busy season of pruning white oaks and planting rice seedlings was just around the corner. If I refused to work and went back home, he'd be in trouble. Around this time last year, he threw a rock at me for sleeping in late after I'd complained a little and sprained my ankle in my sleep. I lay sick in bed for a few days, exaggerating my pain, and he was almost in tears by the end, wasn't he?

"Listen, please get up and work! The only way you'll get to marry is if you work and we have a good harvest this fall, right?"

So, my ears pricked up with surprise, and, to my father-in-law's wide-eyed surprise, I got up then and there and finished leveling and softening rice

내 뺄까 하다가 꾹꾹 참고 말았다.

참말이지 난 이 꼴 하고는 집으로 차마 못 간다. 장가를 들러 갔다가 오죽 못났어야 그대로 쫓겨 왔느냐고 손가락질을 받을 테니까…….

논둑에서 벌떡 일어나 한풀 죽은 장인님 앞으로 다가서며,

"난 갈 테야유, 그동안 사경[17] 쳐내슈 뭐."

"너 사위로 왔지 어디 머슴 살러 왔니?"

"그러면 얼찐 성례를 해줘야 안 하지유. 밤낮 부려만 먹구 해준다 해준다……."

"글세, 내가 안 하는 거냐? 그년이 안 크니까……."
하고 어름어름 담배만 담으면서 늘 하는 소리를 또 늘어놓는다.

이렇게 따져 나가면 언제든지 늘 나만 밑지고 만다. 이번엔 안 된다 하고 대뜸 구장님[18]한테로 단판 가자고 소맷자락을 내끌었다.

"아 이 자식이, 왜 이래 어른을."

안 간다고 뻗디디고 이렇게 호령은 제 맘대로 하지만 장인님 제가 내 기운은 못 당한다. 막 부려먹고 딸은 안 주고, 게다 땅땅 치는 건 다 뭐야…….

paddies that day, which would have normally been a two-day affair. So, then, wouldn't it have been fair for him to have really married us that fall? I was hauling rice bags and gently stacking them in the granary, but all he said, while pointing to Jeom-sun carrying a water jug on her head: "You little—! How could you even say that you want to marry that girl before she grows up, huh?"

After embarrassing me like that, he pretended there was nothing more to discuss. I was so angry that I thought of throwing him down onto the terrace stones and running back to my home village, but I managed to check myself.

Actually, I couldn't go back home like that. I'd be forever scorned for getting kicked out from the family that was supposed to accept me as their son-in-law.

So abruptly I got up from the ridge between rice fields, and strode over to Father-in-law, who was still a little down about everything.

"I'm leaving," I said. "I'll take my total pay now, alright?"

"You came to us as my son-in-law, not as my farm servant, right?"

"If that's the case, you've got to marry us soon.

그러나 내 사실 참 장인님이 미워서 그런 것은 아니다.

그 전날 왜 내가 새고개 맞은 봉우리 화전밭을 혼자 갈고 있지 않았느냐. 밭 가생이로 돌 적마다 야릇한 꽃내가 물컥물컥 코를 찌르고 머리 위에서 벌들은 가끔 붕붕 소리를 친다. 바위틈에서 샘물 소리밖에 안 들리는 산골짜기니까 맑은 하늘의 봄볕은 이불 속같이 따스하고 꼭 꿈꾸는 것 같다. 나는 몸이 나른하고 몸살(을 아직 모르지만 병)이 나려고 그러는지 가슴이 울렁울렁하고 이랬다.

"이러이! 말이! 맘 마 마……."

이렇게 노래를 하며 소를 부리면 여느 때 같으면 어깨가 으쓱으쓱한다. 웬일인지 밭 반도 갈지 않아서 온몸의 맥이 풀리고 대고 짜증만 난다. 공연히 소만 들입다 두들기며,

"안야! 안야! 이 망할 자식의 소(장인님의 소니까) 대리[19]를 꺾어줄라."

그러나 내 속은 정말 안야 때문이 아니라 점심을 이고 온 점순이의 키를 보고 울화가 났던 것이다.

점순이는 뭐 그리 썩 예쁜 계집애는 못 된다. 그렇다

22

You just keep riding me day and night, giving me the same promise over and over again..."

"Well, it's not that I don't want to. It's just that that bitch isn't growing up."

He was just singing the same ambiguous song over and over again, filling his pipe with tobacco.

When we argue like that, it's always me who ends up on the losing side. But I decided then and there, that this time things would be different. I pulled him by the sleeve, insisting that we negotiate through the village headman's arbitration process.

"Ugh, you, how dare you do this to your elder?"

Although he held out and yelled at me as he pleased, he wasn't a match for me in strength. After working me hard and still refusing me his daughter, how dare he yell at me now?

Still, I wasn't acting this way because I hated my father-in-law.

The day before yesterday, I'd tilled a slash-and-burn field alone atop the hill across Sae Ridge, hadn't I? Whenever I turned around the edge of that field, a strange, flowery fragrance pierced my nose and the bees went buzzing over my head. It was a remote mountain area where you can only hear spring water from between rocks. The spring sun

고 개떡이냐 하면 그런 것도 아니고, 꼭 내 아내가 돼야 할 만치 그저 툽툽하게[20] 생긴 얼굴이다. 나보다 십 년 이 아래니까 올해 열여섯인데 몸은 남보다 두 살이나 덜 자랐다. 남은 잘도 훤칠히들 크건만 이건 위아래가 몽톡한 것이 내 눈에는 헐없이[21] 감참외[22] 같다. 참외 중에는 감참외가 제일 맛 좋고 예쁘니까 말이다. 둥글 고 커단 눈은 서글서글하니 좋고, 좀 지쳐 찢어졌지만 입은 밥술이나 톡톡히 먹음직하니 좋다. 아따 밥만 많 이 먹게 되면 팔자는 고만 아니냐. 한데 한 가지 파[23]가 있다면 가끔가다 몸이(장인님은 이걸 채신이 없이 들까분다 고 하지만) 너무 빨리빨리 논다. 그래서 밥을 나르다가 때 없이 풀밭에서 깻박을 쳐서[24] 흙투성이 밥을 곧잘 먹인다. 안 먹으면 무안해할까 봐서 이걸 섭고 앉았노 라면 으적으적 소리만 나고 돌을 먹는 겐지 밥을 먹는 겐지…….

그러나 이날은 웬일인지 성한 밥째로 밭머리에 곱게 내려놓았다. 그리고 또 내외를 해야 하니까 저만큼 떨 어져 이쪽으로 등을 향하고 웅크리고 앉아서 그릇 나기 를 기다린다.

내가 다 먹고 물러섰을 때 그릇을 와서 챙기는데, 그

24

in the clear sky seemed to cover me like a comforter. It was warm and like a dream. I felt as if I was getting ill from fatigue (although I wasn't sure if it was really an illness).

"Eoreoyi! Mari! Mam ma ma..."

If I sang like that and work my cow, ordinarily I would dance with my shoulders moving up and down. But for some reason, I felt dispirited and irritated before I even finished half of the tilling work. So, I beat innocent cow and said, "Anya! Anya! You rotten cow (because she was Father-in-law's), I'll break your legs."

But I was angry not really with Anya, but because I saw how small Jeom-sun still was when she brought me my lunch atop her head.

Jeom-sun isn't all that beautiful a girl. But, she's not so ugly, either. Her face is uncouth, just right for my wife. She's ten years younger than me, so she turned sixteen this year. But her body looks two years younger than other girls her age. Unlike others who grow tall and up, she looks, to me, exactly like a ripe persimmon melon, with a round blunt top and bottom. And persimmon melons are the prettiest and most delicious of all the melons. Her big, round eyes look sweet and gentle, and her

런데 난 깜짝 놀라지 않았느냐. 고개를 푹 숙이고 밥함지에 그릇을 포개면서 날더러 들으라는지 혹은 제 소린지,

"밤낮 일만 하다 말 텐가!"

하고 혼자 쫑알거린다. 고대 잘 내외하다가 이게 무슨 소린가, 하고 난 정신이 얼떨떨했다. 그러면서도 한편 무슨 좋은 수나 있는가 싶어서 나도 공중을 대고 혼잣말로,

"그럼 어떡해?"

하니까,

"성례 시켜달라지 뭘 어떡해."

하고 되알지게 쏘아붙이고 얼굴이 발개져서 산으로 그저 도망질을 친다.

나는 잠시 동안 어떻게 되는 심판[25]인지 맥을 몰라서 그 뒷모양만 덤덤히 바라보았다.

봄이 되면 온갖 초목이 물이 오르고 싹이 트고 한다. 사람도 아마 그런가 보다, 하고 며칠 내에 부쩍(속으로) 자란 듯싶은 점순이가 여간 반가운 것이 아니다.

이런 걸 멀쩡하게 안직 어리다구 하니까……

우리가 구장님을 찾아갔을 때 그는 싸리문 밖에 있는

mouth, though a little too wide, looks promising, as if she was someone who could really eat. And if you can eat a lot, then that means you're bound to have a great life, right?

But, if I have to point out her weaknesses, she does have one. Sometimes she's a little too hasty in the way she moves (Father-in-law says it's unbecoming how she can be so impulsive). Out of nowhere, she'll trip over a clod of grass while carrying my lunch and spill it all over the fields, which usually ends with her feeding me rice with a healthy serving of mud. When I put it in my mouth in order not to embarrass her, all I do is make chewing noises. I don't know if I'm about to eat mud or rice...

But, that day, she somehow brought my meal to me intact and gently placed it down on a dry end of the field. And then, she squatted some distance away, her back towards me, because we had to keep our distance from each other as a man and a woman, and waited until I finished eating to take the plates and bowls back.

When I finished eating, she came to pick up the plates and bowls. But then she suddenly surprised me, didn't she? While laying plates and bowls on top of each other in the wooden lunch bowl, she

돼지우리에서 죽을 퍼주고 있었다. 서울엘 좀 갔다 오더니 사람은 점잖아야 한다고 윗수염이(얼른 보면 지붕 위에 앉은 제비 꼬랑지 같다) 양쪽으로 뾰족이 뻗치고 그걸 에헴, 하고 늘 쓰다듬는 손버릇이 있다. 우리를 멀뚱히 쳐다보고 미리 알아챘는지,

"왜 일들 허다 말구 그래?"

하더니 손을 올려서 그 에헴을 한번 후딱 했다.

"구장님! 우리 장인님과 츰에 계약하기를……."

먼저 덤비는 장인님을 뒤로 떠다밀고 내가 허둥지둥 달려들다가 가만히 생각하고,

"아니 우리 빙장[26]님과 츰에."

하고 첫 번부터 다시 말을 고쳤다. 장인님은 빙장님 해야 좋아하고 밖에 나와서 장인님 하면 괜스레 골을 내려구 든다. 뱀두 뱀이래야 좋냐구 창피스러우니 남 듣는 데는 제발 빙장님, 빙모[27]님, 하라구 일상 말조짐[28]을 받아오면서 난 그것도 자꾸 잊는다. 당장도 장인님 하다 옆에서 내 발등을 꾹 밟고 곁눈질을 흘기는 바람에야 겨우 알았지만…….

구장님도 내 이야기를 자세히 듣더니 퍽 딱한 모양이었다. 하기야 구장님뿐만 아니라 누구든지 다 그럴 게

28

muttered under her breath, "Gonna just work day and night and do nothing else, aren't you!"

It wasn't clear whether she had meant to say that me or just to herself. What was this after keeping such good distance from me? I was downright confused. Still, wondering if there was any good way out of our plight that she was thinking of, I muttered to the air, "And so what am I supposed to do, then?"

"Just ask him to marry us, what else?"

And with that fierce retort, she just ran away to the hills, her face flushed.

For a while, I didn't understand what was going on and just looked her back without saying another word.

In the spring, the sap of every plant and tree rises out of the ground and send out its sprouts. People might not be all that different. With that thought in mind, I was pretty happy to see Jeom-sun grown (inside, at least) in just a few days.

He still calls this girl young. Shameless...

When we went to see the village headman, he was feeding pigs at the pigsty outside of the bush clover gate of his house. After his visit to Seoul, he'd developed the habit of passing his hand over his

다. 길게 길러 둔 새끼손톱으로 코를 후벼서 저리 탁 튀기며,

"그럼 봉필 씨! 얼른 성례를 시켜주구려, 그렇게까지 제가 하구 싶다는 걸……."

하고 내 짐작대로 말했다. 그러나 이 말에 장인님이 삿대질로 눈을 부라리고,

"아 성례구 뭐구 계집애 년이 미처 자라야 할 게 아닌가?"

하니까 고만 멀쑤룩해서 입맛만 쩍쩍 다실 뿐이 아닌가.

"그것두 그래!"

"그래, 거진 사 년 동안에도 안 자랐다니 그 킨 은제 자라지유? 다 그만두구 사경 내슈……."

"글쎄, 이 자식아! 내가 크질 말라구 그랬니, 왜 날 보구 떼냐?"

"빙모님은 참새만 한 것이 그럼 어떻게 앨 났지유?(사실 장모님은 점순이보다도 귀때기 하나가 작다)"

장인님은 이 말을 듣고 껄껄 웃더니(그러나 암만해두 돌쩌귀은 상이다) 코를 푸는 척하고 날 은근히 굻리려고 팔꿈치로 옆갈비께를 퍽 치는 것이다. 더럽다. 나도 종아리

30

handlebar mustache (at first glance, it looks like a swallowtail atop a roof), claiming that people needed to be more dignified. "Ahem," he'd say. Perhaps he realized why we came after staring at us for a while. "What's the matter?" he said. "Shouldn't you two be working?"

And then he raised his hand and quickly did his "Ahem" thing.

"Mr. Village Headman, sir! In the beginning my contract with Father-in-law was..."I'd just muscled Father-in-law out of the way, and was hurrying to make my point, when I thought again and corrected myself: "Excuse me, in the beginning my contract with my *honorable* father-in-law was..."

Father-in-law didn't like me calling him "Father-in-law." He'd get angry with me for no reason and say he preferred me calling him "my honorable father-in-law." Although he continues to harass me about it, protesting that even a snake doesn't like to be called a snake, and says that I should call him and Mother-in-law "my honorable father-in-law" and "my honorable mother-in-law" in front of others, because it's embarrassing otherwise, I keep forgetting. Even at that moment, I only realized my mistake because he was stepping on my foot and

의 파리를 쫓는 척하고 허리를 구부리며 어깨로 그 궁둥이를 꽉 떼밀었다. 장인님은 앞으로 우찔근하고 싸리문께로 쓰러질 듯하다 몸을 바로 고치더니 눈총을 몹시 쏘았다. 이런 쌍년의 자식! 하곤 싶으나 남의 앞이라서 차마 못 하고 섰는 그 꼴이 보기에 퍽 쟁그라웠다.[29)

그러나 이 말에는 별반 신통한 귀정[30)을 얻지 못하고 도로 논으로 돌아와서 모를 부었다. 왜냐면 장인님이 뭐라고 귓속말로 수군수군하고 간 뒤다. 구장님이 날 위해서 조용히 데리고 아래와 같이 일러주었기 때문이다(뭉태의 말은 구장님이 장인님에게 땅 두 마지기 얻어 부치니까 그래 꾀었다고 하지만 난 그렇게 생각하지 않는다).

"자네 말두 하기야 옳지, 암 나이 찼으니까 아들이 급하다는 게 잘못된 말은 아니야. 허지만 농사가 한창 바쁠 때 일을 안 한다든가 집으로 달아난다든가 하면 손해죄루 그것두 징역을 가거든! (여기에 그만 정신이 번쩍 났다) 왜 요전에 삼포말서 산에 불 좀 놓았다구 징역 간 거 못 봤나? 제 산에 불을 놓아두 징역을 가는 이땐데 남의 농사를 버려주니 죄가 얼마나 더 중한가. 그리고 자넨 정장[31)을(사경 받으러 정장 가겠다 했다) 간대지만 그러면 괜시리 죄를 들쓰고 들어가는 걸세. 또 결혼두 그렇지,

scowling at me...

After listening to my story carefully, the village headman looked very sorry for me indeed. And who wouldn't? Everyone else, not just the village headman, would feel pretty bad for me. After picking his nose with his pinky, the nail of which he grew long on purpose, and then flipping the dried mucus away, he said, as I expected: "So, Master Bong-pil! Why don't you go ahead and marry them, then? He wants it so desperately."

But Father-in-law just glared at him, and growled: "But the girl's gotta grow up first if she wants a marriage, or something, doesn't she?"

Then, what else could the village headman do but just smack his lips, embarrassed?

"That's true!" he agreed.

"But, if she hasn't grown for almost four years, when will she get big enough? Just forget it and pay me my wages then!"

"My, you—you—! Did I tell her not to grow? Why are you throwing tantrum at me?"

"So, how did my honorable mother-in-law, who's as small as a sparrow, end up with Father-in-law and bearing a child? (Mother-in-law's shorter than Jeom-sun by the length of an ear).

법률에 성년이란 게 있는데 스물하나가 돼야지 비로소 결혼을 할 수 있는 걸세. 자넨 물론 아들이 늦을 걸 염려하지만 점순이루 말하면 인제 겨우 열여섯이 아닌가. 그렇지만 아까 빙장님의 말씀이 올 갈에는 열 일을 제치고라두 성례를 시켜주겠다 하시니 좀 고마울 겐가. 빨리 가서 모 붓던 거나 마저 붓게, 군소리 말구 어서 가."

그래서 오늘 아침까지 끽소리 없이 왔다.

장인님과 내가 싸운 것은 지금 생각하면 뜻밖의 일이라 안 할 수 없다. 장인님으로 말하면 요즈막 작인들에게 행세를 좀 하고 싶다고 해서

"돈 있으면 양반이지 별게 있느냐!"

하고 일부러 아랫배를 툭 내밀고 걸음도 뒤틀리게 걷고 하는 이 판이다. 이까짓 나쯤 뚜들기다 남의 땅을 가지고 모처럼 닦아놓았던 가문을 망친다든지 할 어른이 아니다. 또 나로 논지면[32] 아무쪼록 잘 봬서 점순이에게 얼른 장가를 들어야 하지 않느냐.

이렇게 말하자면 결국 어젯밤 뭉태네 집에 마실 간 것이 썩 나빴다. 낮에 구장님 앞에서 장인님과 내가 싸운 것을 어떻게 알았는지 대고 빈정거리는 것이 아닌

Father-in-law laughed loudly at this—still, he looked like someone who just swallowed a stone— and then gave me a sharp elbow in the ribs while pretending to blow his nose. The nerve! So, pretending to shoo away a fly from my calf, I bent over and shoved him hard from behind with my shoulder. Father-in-law whirled around, almost bumping into the bush clover gate in the process, and then stood up straight to glare at me. I felt great satisfaction seeing him unable to call me a "son-of-a-bitch!" or something worse. After all, we were still in front of the village headman.

But, in the end, I still had to return without achieving any of my intended results and go back to planting the rice seedlings. Father-in-law had left after whispering something to the village headman's ear, and then the village headman had serenely delivered his judgment, for my sake. (Although, Mung-tae thought his final words weren't at all for me. More for the two stakes of land he was farming for Father-in-law. But I don't think that's the case).

"What you said was right, too, in fact. It's not wrong to be in a hurry to have a son at your age. But, if you don't work or if you run back home during a busy farming season, you might have to go to jail for

35

가.

"그래 맞구두 그걸 가만둬?"

"그럼 어떡하니?"

"임마, 봉필일 모판에다 거꾸루 박아놓지 뭘 어떡해?"
하고 괜히 내 대신 화를 내 가지고 주먹질을 하다 등잔
까지 쳤다. 놈이 본시 괄괄은 하지만 그래 놓고 날더러
석윳값을 물라고 막 지다위[33]를 붓는다. 난 어안이 벙벙
해서 잠자코 앉았으니까 저만 연방 지껄이는 소리가,

"밤낮 일만 해주구 있을 테냐?"

"영득이는 일 년을 살구두 장갈 들었는데 난 사 년이
나 살구두 더 살아야 해?"

"네가 세 번째 사원 줄이나 아니? 세 번째 사위."

"남의 일이라두 분하다 이 자식아, 우물에 가 빠져 죽
어."

나중에는 겨우 손톱으로 목을 따라고까지 하고 제 아
들같이 함부로 훅닥이었다.[34] 별의별 소리를 다 해서 그
대로 옮길 수는 없으나 그 줄거리는 이렇다.

우리 장인님이 딸이 셋이 있는데 맏딸은 재작년 가을
에 시집을 갔다. 정말은 시집을 간 것이 아니라 그 딸도
데릴사위를 해 가지고 있다가 내보냈다. 그런데 딸이

damages! (I was alarmed by this.) Haven't you heard of
the man from Sampo village who was sent to prison for burning his own mountain forest? Now you
can go to prison for burning your own forest, so
how much more serious do you think it'll be to ruin
someone else's harvest? And, you say you'd make a
petition at the governmental office—I did say that I'd
petition at the governmental office to get my wages—but you'd be exposing your own crimes, too!
Besides, as for the legal age for marriage, you have
to be twenty-one. Of course, you're worried that
you'll have a son late, but Jeom-sun's only sixteen
now, isn't she? And yet, your honorable father-in-
law told me just now that he'd marry you this fall no
matter what! You should be grateful! Now why don't
you hurry on back and finish planting those rice
seedlings, and now if you can! Say no more! Off
you go!"

So I hadn't complained at all until this morning.

In retrospect, my fight with Father-in-law was
quite unexpected. Father-in-law was the kind of
man who really liked to strut in front of the tenant
farmers. He liked to put on airs. He'd thrust his belly forward, and say: "Aristocrats are those with
money—and no one else!" He is not the one who'd

열 살 때부터 열아홉, 즉 십 년 동안에 데릴사위를 갈아들이기를, 동리에선 사위 부자라고 이름이 났지마는 열네 놈이란 참 너무 많다. 장인님이 아들은 없고 딸만 있는 고로 그담 딸을 데릴사위를 해올 때까지는 부려먹지 않으면 안 된다. 물론 머슴을 두면 좋지만 그건 돈이 드니까, 일 잘하는 놈을 고르느라고 연방 바꿔 들였다. 또 한편 놈들이 욕만 줄창 퍼붓고 심히도 부려먹으니까 밸이 상해서 달아나기도 했겠지. 점순이는 둘째 딸인데 내가 일테면 그 세 번째 데릴사위로 들어온 셈이다. 내 담으로 네 번째 놈이 들어올 것을 내가 일도 참 잘하고 그리고 사람이 좀 어수룩하니까 장인님이 잔뜩 붙들고 놓질 않는다. 셋째 딸이 인제 여섯 살, 적어두 열 살은 돼야 데릴사위를 할 테므로 그동안은 죽도록 부려먹어야 된다. 그러니 인제는 속 좀 차리고 장가를 들여 달라구 떼를 쓰고 나자빠져라, 이것이다.

나는 건성으로 엉, 엉, 하며 귓등으로 들었다. 뭉태는 땅을 얻어 부치다가 떨어진 뒤로는 장인님만 보면 공연히 못 먹어서 으릉거린다. 그것도 장인님이 저 달라고 할 적에 제집에서 위한다는 그 감투(예전에 원님이 쓰던 것이라나, 옆구리에 뽕뽕 좀먹은 걸레)를 선뜻 주었더라면

38

end up ruining his own family—his family, which he'd worked so hard to build up by managing someone else's land—just to squash a small fly like me. As for me, I really should have been trying to get on his good side so that I could marry Jeom-sun soon, shouldn't I have?

Given all of this, it was, after all, probably not such a great thing for me to visit Mung-tae last night. I wonder how he'd heard about it, but he immediately sneered at me for arguing with Father-in-law in front of the village headman. He did indeed.

"So, you got slapped, and just gave up, huh?"

"And what else could I have done?"

"You, idiot, what else but toss Bong-pil head first onto a seed-plot?"

He looked furious on my behalf, and even brandished his fist, knocking his own lamp over in the end. Mung-tae was hot-tempered, alright. He even insisted that I pay for his spilled lamp oil. While I just sat there to that, dumbfounded, he started at it again:

"So you're gonna just work for him, day and night?"

"Whereas Yeong-deuk got married after only a year, you have to work more even after four years.

그럴 리도 없었던 걸…….

그러나 나는 뭉태란 놈의 말을 전수이[35] 곧이듣지 않
았다. 꼭 곧이들었다면 간밤에 와서 장인님과 싸웠지
무사히 있었을 리가 없지 않은가. 그러면 딸에게까지
인심을 잃은 장인님이 혼자 나빴다.

실토이지 나는 점순이가 아침상을 가지고 나올 때까
지는 오늘은 또 얼마나 밥을 담았나, 하고 이것만 생각
했다. 상에는 된장찌개하고 간장 한 종지, 조밥 한 그릇,
그리고 밥보다 더 수부룩하게 담은 산나물이 한 대접,
이렇다. 나물은 점순이가 틈틈이 해 오니까 두 대접이
고 네 대접이고 멋대로 먹어도 좋으나 밥은 장인님이
한 사발 외엔 더 주지 말라고 해서 안 된다. 그런데 점순
이가 그 상을 내 앞에 내려놓으며 제 말로 지껄이는 소
리가,

"구장님한테 갔다 그냥 온담 그래!"

하고 엊그제 산에서와 같이 되우 좋알거린다. 딴은 내
가 더 단단히 덤비지 않고 만 것이 좀 어리석었다. 속으
로 그랬다. 나도 저쪽 벽을 향하여 외면하면서 내 말로,

"안 된다는 걸 그럼 어떡헌담!"

하니까,

Right?"

"You know you're his third son-in-law, don't you?"

"I'm angry even though it's none of my business! You right fool! Go drown yourself in the well!"

In the end, he even told me I should use my own fingernail to cut my throat, harassing me as if I were his son. Although I can't say everything he told me, because he said so many ridiculous things, I can summarize it as follows:

Father-in-law has three daughters, and the first daughter was married off two years ago. Actually, she wasn't really married off at all, but Father took son-in-law in and then sent him and her away after marrying them. But, in the meantime, he went through as many as fourteen sons-in-law from his daughter's tenth to nineteenth birthday. Ten years of sons-in-law. Although everyone knows Father-in-law has quite a few sons-in-law amongst the village, fourteen was something else. And since Father-in-law doesn't have a son, only daughters, he has to work his son-in-law for the hand of his first daughter until he can replace him with a son-in-law waiting in line for his second daughter. Of course, he could hire a farm servant, but that would

"쇰[36]을 잡아채지 그냥 둬, 이 바보야?"

하고 또 얼굴이 빨개지면서 성을 내며 안으로 샐쭉하니 튀 들어가지 않느냐. 이때 아무도 본 사람이 없었게 망정이지 보았다면 내 얼굴이 에미 잃은 황새 새끼처럼 가엾다 했을 것이다.

사실 이때만치 슬펐던 일이 또 있었는지 모른다. 다른 사람은 암만 못생겼다 해도 괜찮지만 내 아내 될 점순이가 병신으로 본다면 참 신세는 따분하다. 밥을 먹은 뒤 지게를 지고 일터로 가려 하다 도로 벗어 던지고 바깥마당 공석[37] 위에 드러누워서 나는 차라리 죽느니만 같지 못하다 생각했다.

내가 일 안 하면 장인님 저는 나이가 먹어 못 하고 결국 농사 못 짓고 만다. 뒷짐으로 트림을 꿀꺽, 하고 대문 밖으로 나오다 날 보고서,

"이 자식아! 너 왜 또 이러니?"

"관객[38]이 났어유, 아이구 배야!"

"기껏 밥 처먹고 나서 무슨 관객이야, 남의 농사 버려 주면 이 자식아 징역 간다 봐라!"

"가두 좋아유, 아이구 배야!"

참말 난 일 안 해서 징역 가도 좋다 생각했다. 일후[39]

42

cost more. So, he keeps changing his first son-in-law until he finds one who works well. Also, some had just run away because they were pissed on account of the name-calling and workload. Jeom-sun was his second daughter and I was so-to-speak his third, second son-in-law. He hadn't replaced me with his fourth, because I worked so hard and was utterly naïve. He was holding onto me hard. His third daughter was only six years old now, so he has to work me to death until she becomes ten, which is when he might consider son-in-law for her hand. In conclusion, I needed to wake up this instant and insist on our marriage no matter what. That was what he told me.

I didn't pay much attention to what he said. I mostly just smiled and nodded my head. Since Mung-tae had lost his tenancy, he'd been growling at my father-in-law at every possible occasion, as if he wanted to swallow him alive. He wouldn't have lost his tenancy if he'd willingly given my father-in-law the horsehair cap (a rag, the side of which was eaten by worms and which he claims a local governor used to wear), his family treasure, when my father-in-law asked for it...

But I didn't believe most of what Mung-tae had

아들을 낳아도 그 앞에서 바보 바보 이렇게 별명을 들을 테니까 오늘은 열 쪽이 난대도 결정을 내고 싶었다.

장인님이 일어나라고 해도 내가 안 일어나니까 눈에 독이 올라서 저편으로 힝 하게 가더니 지게막대기를 들고 왔다. 그리고 그걸로 내 허리를 마치 돌 떠넘기듯이 쿡 찍어서 넘기고 넘기고 했다. 밥을 잔뜩 먹고 딱딱한 배가 그럴 적마다 퉁겨지면서 밸창⁴⁰⁾이 꼿꼿한 것이 여간 켕기지 않았다. 그래도 안 일어나니까 이번엔 배를 지게막대기로 위에서 쿡쿡 찌르고 발길로 옆구리를 차고 했다. 장인님은 원체 심청⁴¹⁾이 궂어서 그러지만 나도 저만 못하지 않게 배를 채었다. 아픈 것을 눈을 꽉 감고 넌 해라 난 재미난 듯이 있었으나 볼기짝을 후려갈길 적에는 나도 모르는 결에 벌떡 일어나서 그 수염을 잡아챘다마는 내 골이 난 것이 아니라 정말은 아까부터 부엌 뒤 울타리 구멍으로 점순이가 우리들의 꼴을 몰래 엿보고 있었기 때문이다. 가뜩이나 말 한마디 톡톡히 못 한다고 바보라는데 매까지 잠자코 맞는 걸 보면 짜장 바보로 알 게 아닌가. 또 점순이도 미워하는 이까짓 놈의 장인님, 나하곤 아무것도 안 되니까 막 때려도 좋지만 사정 보아서 수염만 채고(제 원대로 했으니까 이때 점

44

said. If I had, then wouldn't I have argued with Father-in-law that night after I had returned home instead of keeping quiet? Considering all these, Father-in-law, whom even his own daughter doesn't like, was alone to be blamed.

Honestly, until Jeom-sun brought breakfast today, the only thing I wondered about was how much rice she'd bring. There was a bowl of *doenjang* stew, a small bowl of soy sauce, a bowl of boiled rice with millet, and a bowl heaped with wild edible greens higher than the rice on the table. Although I could have as many bowls of wild edible greens as I wanted—two bowls or four bowls, even—rice was a different matter. Father-in-law had ordered to give me no more than one bowl. At any rate, as she brought the breakfast table to me, Jeom-sun muttered fiercely, like she had in the mountain fields the day before yesterday: "What's the use of going to the village headman if you come back with nothing!"

Come to think of it, I had been rather stupid when I hadn't fought more aggressively. I thought about this. I looked at the wall, away from Jeom-sun, and said: "What could I do when he insisted!"

"Why not grab him by the mustache instead of

순이는 퍽 기뻤겠지) 저기까지 잘 들리도록,

"이걸 까셀라<sup>42)</sup> 부다!"

하고 소리를 쳤다.

장인님은 더 약이 바짝 올라서 잡은 참 지게막대기로 내 어깨를 그냥 내리갈겼다. 정신이 다 아찔하다. 다시 고개를 들었을 때 그때엔 나도 온몸에 약이 올랐다. 이 녀석의 장인님을, 하고 눈에서 불이 퍽 나서 그 아래 밭 있는 낭<sup>43)</sup> 아래로 그대로 떠밀어 굴려버렸다. 조금 있다가 장인님이 씩씩 하고 한번 해 보려고 기어오르는 걸 얼른 또 떠밀어 굴려버렸다.

기어오르면 굴리고, 굴리면 기어오르고, 이러길 한 너덧 번을 하며 그럴 적마다,

"부려만 먹구 왜 성례 안 하지유!"

나는 이렇게 호령했다. 하지만 장인님이 선뜻, 오냐 닐이라두 성례시켜 주마, 했으면 나도 성가신 걸 그만두었을지 모른다. 나야 이러면 때린 건 아니니까 나중에 장인 쳤다는 누명도 안 들을 터이고 얼마든지 해도 좋다.

한번은 장인님이 헐떡헐떡 기어서 올라오더니 내 바짓가랑이를 요렇게 노리고서 단박 움켜잡고 매달렸다.

just leaving him alone, you fool?"

Then, wouldn't you know it—but she blushed a bright red, glared at me, and tore off in the direction of house. Thank goodness, nobody saw me then, because if anybody did, he would have certainly pitied me. I must have looked like a stork chick who'd just lost its mother.

In fact, I don't know if I have ever been as sad as I was then. It didn't matter if anyone else called me a fool, but if Jeom-sun, my wife to be, saw me that way, that was a truly pitiful situation. After breakfast, I took an A-frame carrier to lug to work when I thought better of it, tossed it aside, and crumpled down onto an empty sack. I felt like dying would be better than being in the situation I was in.

If I didn't work, Father-in-law couldn't work the farm by himself; he was too old. He noticed me lying down on his way out the gate. He was walking with his hands clasped behind his back, burping. Immediately, he began to spit, "Damn you! What's the matter with you?"

"I've got a stomachache. Oh my stomach!"

"What stomachache? And after shoveling down all that precious rice? If you want to ruin my farm, you'll find yourself behind some prison doors! Wait and

악, 소리를 치고 나는 그만 세상이 다 팽그르 도는 것이,

"빙장님! 빙장님! 빙장님!"

"이 자식! 잡아먹어라. 잡아먹어!"

"아! 아! 할아버지! 살려 줍쇼, 할아버지!"

하고 두 팔을 허둥지둥 내절 적에는 이마에 진땀이 쭉 내솟고 인젠 참으로 죽나 보다, 했다. 그래도 장인님은 놓질 않더니 내가 기어이 땅바닥에 쓰러져서 거진 까무러치게 되니까 놓는다. 더럽다, 더럽다. 이게 장인님인가, 나는 한참을 못 일어나고 쩔쩔맸다. 그러다 얼굴을 드니(눈에 참 아무것도 보이지 않았다) 사지가 부르르 떨리면서 나도 엉금엉금 기어가 장인님의 바짓가랑이를 꽉 움키고 잡아 나꿨다.

내가 머리가 터지도록 매를 얻어맞은 것이 이 때문이다. 그러나 여기가 또한 우리 장인님이 유달리 착한 곳이다. 여느 사람이면 사경을 주어서라도 당장 내쫓았지 터진 머리를 불솜[44]으로 손수 지져주고, 호주머니에 희연[45] 한 봉을 넣어주시고 그리고,

"올 갈엔 꼭 성례를 시켜주마. 암말 말구 가서 뒷골의 콩밭이나 얼른 갈아라."

하고 등을 뚜덕여 줄 사람이 누구냐.

see!"

"I don't care—oh my stomach!"

And at that moment, I really thought that I didn't care if I ended up in prison from not working. Even if I had a son later on, someone would still call me a fool. I wanted to settle my matters today no matter what.

When I didn't get up even after Father-in-law ordered me to, he rushed to the other side of the yard, a mad look in his eyes, and returned with an A-frame carrier pole. And then, he poked and turned my body over with it as if he was turning over a rock. Whenever he poked my belly, taut and full with breakfast (I'd eaten to my heart's content), my belly bounced hard and extremely uncomfortably. But I still wouldn't get up, and so he then proceeded to poke me not only in my belly from above, but also to kick me in my sides with his feet. Although I expected this because of Father-in-law's famously hot temper, I didn't back down at all. Although it was extremely painful, I withstood it all, as if I was enjoying his poking and kicking. It wasn't until finally he began to thrash my buttocks that I automatically shot upright and grabbed him by his mustache. I did this, though, not because I was angry,

나는 장인님이 너무나 고마워서 어느덧 눈물까지 났다. 점순이를 남기고 이젠 내쫓기려니, 하다 뜻밖의 말을 듣고,

"빙장님! 인제 다시는 안 그러겠어유."

이렇게 맹세를 하며 부랴사랴[46] 지게를 지고 일터로 갔다.

그러나 이때는 그걸 모르고 장인님을 원수로만 여겨서 잔뜩 잡아당겼다.

"아! 아! 이놈아! 놔라, 놔."

장인님은 헛손질을 하며 솔개미[47]에 챈 닭의 소리를 연해 질렀다. 놓긴 왜, 이왕이면 호되게 혼을 내주리라, 생각하고 짓궂이 더 댕겼다마는 장인님이 땅에 쓰러져서 눈에 눈물이 피잉 도는 것을 알고 좀 겁도 났다.

"할아버지! 놔라, 놔, 놔, 놔놔."

그래도 안 되니까,

"애 점순아! 점순아!"

이 악장[48]에 안에 있었던 장모님과 점순이가 헐레벌떡하고 단숨에 뛰어나왔다.

나의 생각에 장모님은 제 남편이니까 역성을 하는지도 모른다. 그러나 점순이는 내 편을 들어서 속으로 고

but because Jeom-sun had, in fact, been secretly watching us the whole time from behind the kitchen and through a hole in the fence. If she already thought me a fool for not arguing better earlier, wouldn't she think me a real fool if she thought I'd let him beat me without fighting back? Also, although I could have beaten Father-in-law to a pulp, and even Jeom-sun hated him, I decided to just grab him by his mustache (I guess Jeom-sun must have been happy because I did what she wanted). I hollered loud so that she could hear me well: "I can beat you to a pulp if I want to!"

Even more incensed, Father-in-law hit me over my shoulder with the carrier pole. I felt dizzy. As I looked up, it seemed like my entire body seized with anger. My eyes fiery, and cursing him under my breath, I pushed him down a low hill of fields. When he clambered back up the hill, panting, ready to fight again, I gave him a quick shove back down the hill.

He took four or five tumbles, and every time he tried to clamber up, I yelled at him: "Why do you just keep working me? Why won't you give me my wedding?"

If, by his own will, he said, Okay, I'll throw a wed-

소해서 하겠지. 대체 이게 웬 속인지(지금까지도 난 영문을 모른다) 아버질 혼내 주기는 제가 내래 놓고 이제 와서는 달려들며,

"에그머니! 이 망할 게 아버지 죽이네!"

하고 내 귀를 뒤로 잡아당기며 마냥 우는 것이 아니냐. 그만 여기에 기운이 탁 꺾이어 나는 얼빠진 등신이 되고 말았다. 장모님도 덤벼들어 한쪽 귀마저 뒤로 잡아채면서 또 우는 것이다.

이렇게 꼼짝 못 하게 해놓고 장인님은 지게막대기를 들어서 사뭇 내리조겼다.[49] 그러나 나는 구태여 피하려지도 않고 암만해도 그 속 알 수 없는 점순이의 얼굴만 멀거니 들여다보았다.

"이 자식! 장인 입에서 할아버지 소리가 나오도록 해?"

1) 과연 정말로.
2) 어리둥절하여 갈피를 잡을 수 없이 멍하다.
3) 모를 붓다. 못자리를 만들어 씨를 뿌리다.
4) 거불지다. 둥글고 두두룩하게 툭 비어져 나오다.
5) 속병. 위장병.
6) '숱'의 방언. 머리털 따위의 부피나 분량.
7) 세워 놓고.
8) 지주를 대리하여 소작권을 관리하는 사람.
9) 뼈대가 굵고 털이 북슬북슬한 개.
10) 소작인.

ding for you right away. Tomorrow even! I would have stopped pushing him down right then. It was becoming bothersome anyway. It wasn't a big deal for me to keep doing it, though; no one would blame me for beating up Father-in-law just for pushing him down over and over.

Then, Father-in-law clambered up, puffing and blowing and aiming for my thing, and then he reached out and got a hold of it. I screamed as the world began to spin.

"Honorable father-in-law! Honorable father-in-law! Honorable father-in-law!"

"You son-of-a-bitch! You wanna kill me, don't you?"

"Ah! Ah! Grandfather! Please let me live, Grandfather!"

I swung my arms helter-skelter, pouring sweat from my forehead and on down, and thinking that I was really going to die. Even then, Father-in-law didn't let it go until I collapsed to the ground and almost passed out. How crude! How crude! Could this be Father-in-law? Entirely flustered, I couldn't get up for a long time. Then, when I finally was able to raise my head (I couldn't see anything by the way) I was furious and I crawled towards him and

11) 여러 번의 김매기 중 첫 김매기를 한 논.
12) 몹시 속을 태우며 여기저기로 다니는 사람.
13) 남의 것을 빼돌려 가지다.
14) 갈참나무 잎.
15) 논을 삶다. 논밭의 흙을 써레로 썰고 나래로 골라 노글노글하게 만들다.
16) 비위에 거슬리거나 마음이 언짢아서 성이 나는 김.
17) 주인이 머슴에게 주는 한 해 농사일의 대가.
18) 예전에 시골 동네의 우두머리를 이르던 말.
19) '다리'의 방언.
20) 생김새가 멋이 없고 투박하다.
21) 영락없이.
22) 속이 잘 익은 감같이 붉고 맛이 좋다.
23) 결점.
24) 깻박치다. 그릇 따위를 떨어뜨려 속에 있던 것이 산산이 흩어지게 만들다.
25) '셈판'의 방언. 셈을 놓는 데 쓰는 수판.
26) 다른 사람의 장인(丈人)을 이르는 말.
27) 다른 사람의 장모를 이르는 말.
28) 말조심.
29) 쟁그랍다. 미운 사람이 실수하여 몹시 고소하다.
30) 그릇되었던 일이 바른길로 돌아옴. 여기서는 판결.
31) 소장(訴狀)을 관청에 냄.
32) 말하자면.
33) 남에게 등을 대고 의지하거나 떼를 씀.
34) 공연한 말로 꼴사납게 지껄이다.
35) 모두.
36) '수염'의 방언.
37) 아무것도 담지 않은 빈 섬. 섬은 곡식 따위를 담기 위하여 짚으로 엮어 만든 그릇.
38) 관격. 먹은 음식이 갑자기 체하여 가슴 속이 막히고 위로는 계속 토하며 아래로는 대소변이 통하지 않는 위급한 증상.
39) 뒷날.
40) 배알. '창자'의 비속어.
41) '마음보(마음을 쓰는 속 바탕)'의 북한어.
42) 세차게 치다.
43) 낭. '둔덕'의 방언.
44) 상처를 소독하기 위하여 불에 그슬린 솜방망이.

grabbed his thing, with all my might.

That was why I was beaten until my head began to bleed. But, this was where Father-in-law was unusually good-natured. Ordinary people would have kicked me out then and there even if they had to pay me my wages. But my father-in-law pressed down on my head wound with singed cotton himself, put a packet of Huiyeon[3] into my pocket, and patted me on my back, saying: "I'll hold your wedding this fall no matter what. Just go and till the pea patch at the valley behind the house." Who else but my father-in-law would have done that?

I was so grateful to him I was even moved to tears. I was so expecting that I would have to leave Jeom-sun and be kicked out, I rushed to pledge myself to him, "My honorable father-in-law! I'll never do this again!" and went to work with my A-frame carrier.

But that was later. I didn't know this would happen in the moment, and so I considered Father-in-law as my enemy alone and pulled his thing with all my might.

"Ah! Ah! Damn you! Let go, let, go!"

Father-in-law beat the air and screamed like a chicken caught by a kite. Thinking, "why should I

55

45) 일제 강점기 때 나온 담배 이름.
46) 매우 부산하고 급하게 서두르는 모양.
47) 솔개.
48) 악을 쓰며 싸움.
49) 냅다 두들기거나 때리다.

* 작가 고유의 문체나 당시 쓰이던 용어를 그대로 살려 원문에
  최대한 가깝게 표기하고자 하였다. 단, 현재 쓰이지 않는 말이
  나 띄어쓰기는 현행 맞춤법에 맞게 표기하였다.

『동백꽃』, 삼문사, 1938

let go? I'll teach you," I spitefully pulled harder. Still, seeing him collapse on the ground and his eyes fill with tears, I began to feel scared, too.

"Grandfather! Let go, let, go, let go!"

I still didn't let it go, and then, he called, "Jeom-sun, my dear! Jeom-sun!"

At this noisy row, Mother-in-law and Jeom-sun rushed outside.

I expected that Mother-in-law would be on his side as he was her husband, but that Jeom-sun would be on my side, that she would even gloat. But, what the hell—and I still don't know why—after she had told me all about teaching him a lesson, what else did she do but leap atop me, pulling on one of my ears and wailing: "My goodness! This damn idiot is going to kill Father!"

I felt a real fool. Nothing but dispirited and stunned. Mother-in-law also jumped at me, pulling my other ear and crying, too.

After completely disabling me in this way, Father-in-law raised the A-frame carrier pole above his head and gave me real beating. But, I didn't even try to avoid his blows. I just stared blankly at Jeom-sun's face, whose mind I couldn't understand at all.

"Damn you! You made me, your own father-in-law, call you grandfather?" my father-in-law cried.

1) There is a folk belief in Korea that those who are spoken ill of by others live a long life (Translator's note).
2) Chambong is the traditional title for the lowest ranking governmental official (Translator's note).
3) Huiyeon is the name of a cigarette.

Translated by Jeon Seung-hee

# 해설

**Afterword**

# 하층 농민의 유머와 해학

윤대석 (문학평론가)

경춘선을 타고 가다보면 춘천 조금 못 미친 곳에 김유정역이 있다. 한국 최초로 사람 이름을 붙인 이 역에서 내려 조금 걷다보면 동쪽에 솟은 금병산을 바라보는 김유정 문학 마을이 있다. 이곳은 김유정이 태어났고, 또 청년 시기에 귀향하여 농촌 계몽 활동을 벌인 실레 마을이다. 매우 짧은 작가 생활을 통해 그가 열정적으로 쏟아낸 소설의 절반 이상은 이 마을을 배경으로 펼쳐지는데, 교과서에 수록된 「봄·봄」「동백꽃」을 읽고 자란 한국 사람들은 자신들이 사랑하는 작가의 고향을 찾아 오늘도 김유정역에 정차해 기차에서 내린다. 김유정이라는 작가가 오늘날에도 많은 사람들의 사랑을 받

# The Wit and Humor of the Peasants

Yun Dae-seok (literary critic)

On the Seoul-Chuncheon railway line, a few stops before Chuncheon Station, you will find Kim Yu-jeong Station, the first train station in Korea to be named after a person. A short walk from the eponymous station brings you to the Kim Yu-jeong Literature Village, with a commanding view of Mt. Geumbyeong to the east. This is the village of Sille, where Kim was born and led a campaign to enlighten its peasants when he returned home in his youth.

More than half of Kim's stories, produced in a creative burst during his brief writing career, were set in this village. Many Koreans who grew up

고 있는 것은 물론 교과서 때문이지만, 그와 동시에 그가 표현한 기층 민중의 삶과 정서, 언어에 깊은 공감을 느끼기 때문이기도 하다.

김유정 소설 상당수는 농민의 생활을 다루고 있다(도시를 배경으로 한 소설에서도 하층민이 그 주인공이다). 농민 가운데에서도 하층민의 삶이 그가 주목한 곳이다. 가을이 되어 수확을 해도 지주에게 세를 바치고 빚을 갚고 나면 한줌의 곡식도 남지 않는 소작인, 소작을 붙이는 것도 여의치 않아 여기저기 떠돌아다니며 사는 사람, 남편의 무능력으로 가난한 농민들에게 몸을 팔아 생계를 이어갈 수밖에 없는 들병이 같은 사람들이 그들이다. 그러나 이러한 농촌 하층민의 생활을 다루는 그의 태도는 냉철한 것도 아니고, 울분이나 연민에 차 있는 것이 아니라, 풍자와 해학, 유머를 품고 있다.「봄·봄」은 이러한 풍자와 유머, 해학을 잘 보여주는, 김유정 소설의 대표작이다.

주인공이자 화자인 '나'는 농촌에서 가장 하층에 위치한 사람이다. 그는 땅도 소유하고 있지 않을 뿐만 아니라 소작을 얻는 것조차도 여의치 않고, 아내를 맞이할 만큼 재산도 가지고 있지 않다. 더군다나 얼토당토않은

reading "Spring, Spring" and "Camellias" in the textbooks of their youth disembark at the station to
make a pilgrimage into their beloved writer's
hometown. While their affection springs mainly
from the widespread reprinting of his works in
textbooks, it also stems from his empathy with the
lives of common people, which he captured in their
language and sentiments. Most of his stories deal
with the lives of the peasants. Even those set in cit-
ies revolve around the lives of the lower classes.
After paying rent to their landlord during the autumn harvest, sharecroppers were often left emp-
ty-handed, and so ended up wandering the streets.
Women with inept husbands were forced into
prostitution to make ends meet. Kim's treatment of
the lives of these down-and-out people is neither
cold-hearted nor passionately supportive, but filled
instead with satire, humor, and wit. His representative work, "Spring, Spring," illustrates this attitude.

The protagonist and narrator of this story, the
first-person 'I,' belongs to the lowest rung of society in a country village. He does not own land, is
unable to do sharecropping, and doesn't have
enough money to get married. What's more, he
doesn't have learning or common sense, and so

법률을 들먹이는 구장의 말을 곧이곧대로 믿을 만큼 지식도, 지혜도 가지고 있지 않다. 그가 가진 것은 건장한 몸과 우직한 마음뿐이다. 오로지 몸뚱이뿐인 '나'가 농촌에서 사람답게 살아갈 수 있는 길은, 딸과 결혼시켜 재산을 나눠준다는 장래 장인이 될지도 모르는 봉필의 말을 믿는 것뿐이다.

이에 비해 봉필은 마름이다. 그것도 다른 사람을 괴롭히며 악착같이 돈과 땅을 모은 마름이다. 마름이란 지주를 대신하여 소작인들을 관리하는 임무를 맡은 농촌의 중간 지배층인데, "돈 있으면 양반이지 별게 있느냐"라고 말하는 것에서도 알 수 있듯이 그도 원래 상놈 출신이다. 같은 상놈 출신이면서도 두루 인심을 잃을 정도로 마을 사람들에게 해를 끼치며 자수성가하여 지금과 같은 지위에 오르게 되었다. 그 가운데 돈을 벌기 위해 한 가장 큰 나쁜 짓은 결혼이라는 인륜을 이용해 자신의 이익을 채우고자 한 일이다.

이처럼 이 소설에서는 양반/상놈이라는 구체제적 질서가 무너지고 그것이 식민지 체제하에서 재편된 지주/마름/소작인이라는, 농촌의 새로운 계층적 질서가 반영되어 있다. 이 소설에서 '나'와 마름인 봉필의 대립은 이

falls for the village headman's preposterous claims. What he does possess are a strong physique and a clear conscience. The only way he can preserve his humanity in the countryside is to believe the promise of his reputed future father-in-law, Bong-pil: that the narrator will have his daughter's hand, as well as some of his fortune.

Bong-pil is an overseer of tenant farms, who harasses the unsuspecting and extorts money and land from them. He belongs to the middle class, like other farm foremen who supervise sharecroppers for the landlords. As is revealed by his favorite words, "Aristocrats are those with money—and no one else!" Bong-pil himself was a poor peasant who had managed to make a fortune and climb the social ladder at the expense of his fellow peasants, who feel estranged from him. He is so unscrupulous when it comes to making money that he even exploits marriage customs for his own ends.

The story reflects the new social hierarchy in the countryside, in which the old division between aristocrats and peasants was replaced during the colonial regime with a system of landlords, supervisors, and sharecroppers. The confrontation between Bong-pil and the narrator represents a new

러한 계급적 대립을 의미한다. 그러나 「동백꽃」에서도 묘사된 이러한 계급 문제는 전면에 부각되지 않는다. 그 대신에 이 소설에서 두드러지는 것은 해학과 유머이다. 적절하게 괄호를 사용함으로써 겉모습과 다른 속마음을 표현하거나 앞의 말을 뒤틀거나 하는 방식으로 이 유머는 드러난다. 또한 다른 사람들의 말을 순진하게 믿으면서 터무니없이 용감한 행동에 나서는 '나'의 행동 방식으로도 이 유머는 표현된다. 특히 내외만 하던 점순의 의외의 부추김에 의해 감행하게 된 우직한 행동, 반전의 사건인 점순의 배신에 자포자기하는 심정 등도 독자들에게 웃음을 선사한다. 장인 될 사람과 벌이는 우스꽝스러운 몸싸움은 그러한 유머의 극치라 할 수 있을 것이다. 이러한 유머는 지배 계급의 행동을 풍자함으로써 억압적인 삶을 견디려 한 민중들의 해학 정신이 되었다. 이 소설이 표현하고 있는 것은 한국 기층민들의 해학 정신이다.

이러한 유머는 민중적인 언어와 만남으로써 상승 작용을 일으키는데, 이 점이 번역 작업에서 제대로 전달되기는 어려울 것이다. 이 소설에는 김유정이 자신의 고향 실레마을에서 지내면서 익힌 강원도 하층민의 구

kind of class struggle.

Yet this class issue is never in the foreground in Kim's literature. Rather, wit and humor dominate in his fiction. Characters' inner thoughts are captured in amusing, parenthetical "thought bubbles." Humor is expressed in the narrator's gullibility and bravado despite the ostensibly serious situations. His foolish behavior, at the goading of Jeom-sun, whom he intends to marry when he's permitted, and his despair at her betrayal, elicit the readers' laughter. And a comical scuffle between the narrator and his father-in-law is the story's hysterical humor's culmination. This kind of satirical portrayal of the behavior of the ruling class sums up the spirit of those who endure oppression. Thus, Kim's story captures the humor expressed by those at the bottom of Korean society.

Both the humor and the language spoken by his characters create an overall effect that may be difficult to translate. The colloquial language of the lower classes in Gangwon-do is used in this story, a dialect that Kim learned while growing up and later living in Sille. Some of the words are not found in *The Great Dictionary of Standard Korean* (National Institute of the Korean Language), the most exten-

어가 그대로 재현되어 있다. 그들 일부는 한국에서 가장 큰 사전인 국립국어원의『표준국어대사전』에서도 찾을 수 없을 정도인데, 이를 통해 한국 문학은 언어적 측면에서 더욱더 풍부해졌다고 할 수 있다.

sive language reference in South Korea. As this shows, Kim enriched not only Korea's literature but also its language.

# 비평의 목소리

Critical Acclaim

김유정 자신이 농촌 출신이었기 때문이겠지만 그의
농촌 점묘는 그 누구보다도 탁월하다. 목가적인 사랑을
다루는 초기 걸작들에는 탄력과 활기가 넘쳐난다. 지주
집 자식과 종의 사랑이라는 계층적 대립을 다루고 있으
면서도 살벌한 증오심 대신에 유머가 가득 차 있다. 그
유머는 고전 소설들에서 흔히 볼 수 있는 것이며 그것
이 그를 전통과 굳게 결부시키고 있다.

김현, 「식민지 시대의 재인식과 그 표현」,

김윤식·김현, 『한국문학사』, 민음사, 1973

  김유정의 소설은 가난한 사람들의 삶을 통해 비참한

Hailing from the countryside, Kim Yu-jeong ex-
celled other writers in his portrayal of country life.
His early pastoral romances brim with excitement
and buoyancy. Despite the class conflict inherent in
the love affair between a landlord's daughter and a
servant, his story is filled with humor rather than
hatred. Such humor, also often found in classical
novels, grounds him firmly in the Korean tradition.

Kim Hyun, "A New Understanding of Colonial Period and Its
Expression," Kim Yun-shik and Kim Hyun,
*The History of Korean Literature* (Seoul: Minumsa, 1973).

Kim Yu-jeong's fiction depicts the hardy, inno-

현실의 문제를 비판적으로 그려내는 것이 아니라, 토속적인 구어와 생동하는 문체를 바탕으로 하는 해학과 반어의 기법을 통해, 농민들의 순수한 삶과 끈질긴 생명력을 그려내고 있다. 등장인물들은 대체로 암울한 현실 속에서의 좌절과 분노를 보여주기보다 끈질기게 삶에 집착하는 강한 생존 본능을 드러내고 있다.

권영민, 『한국현대문학사1』, 민음사, 2002


말더듬이였기에 언어 인식에 치열했던 유정이었다. 유정의 날카로운 언어 감각은 고향 사람들이 쓰던 언어를 그대로 작품 속에 생생하게 재생시켰다. 고향 강원도 산골의 가공되지 않은 생생한 언어와 그 속에 스며든 삶의 모습이 작품을 읽는 독자에게 짙은 토속성으로 다가오게 된 것이다.

유인순, 「생명의 길, 문학의 길—김유정의 생애와 문학」,

『김유정과의 동행』, 소명출판, 2014

cent lives of peasants with characteristic irony and humor. His works are written in the native tongue and with a lively style, rather than focusing on the depressing realities of life for the poor. Typically, his characters cling to life, driven by a strong survival instinct, instead of raging and railing against a harsh reality.

Kwon Young-min, *The History of Korean Modern Literature 1*

(Seoul: Minumsa, 2002)

Because he was a stammerer, Kim worked hard to establish his own awareness of language. His acute sense of language is reflected in his works, which capture exactly how his hometown people spoke. The reader discovers a great accomplishment of naiveté in the lively, unrefined language of his village in Gangwon-do and the people's lives celebrated in their own language.

Yoo In-sun, "The Way of Life, The Way of Literature

—Kim Yu-jeong's Life and Literature,"

*Traveling Together With Kim Yu-jeong* (Seoul: Somyong, 2014)

# 김유정

　김유정은 1908년 2월 12일 강원도 춘천시 신동면 증리 실레마을에서 아버지 김춘식, 어머니 심 씨 사이에서 막내로 태어났다. 실레마을 일대의 땅 대부분을 소유한 대지주였던 아버지 김춘식은 김유정이 6살 되던 해 식솔들을 이끌고 서울로 이사한다. 부친이 살아 있는 동안에는 경제적으로 풍족한 삶 속에서 가족들의 사랑을 받고 자란 김유정이었지만, 7살, 9살 부모를 연달아 여의고 난 후, 가독을 승계한 형의 가산 탕진으로, 금전과 사랑에 굶주린 삶을 살게 된다. 나이 차이가 많이 나는 큰 형은 방탕한 생활을 했을 뿐만 아니라 걸핏하면 누이들과 김유정에게 폭력을 행사하였다. 이러한 경험은 김유정에게 커다란 정신적 외상으로 남았는데, 이 점에 대해서는 소설「형(兄)」에 잘 묘사되어 있다.

　재동 보통학교를 졸업한 1923년 휘문 고등보통학교에 진학하여 평생의 친구가 된 소설가 안회남을 만나게 된다. 안회남은 김유정에게 소설 쓰기를 처음 권유했을 뿐만 아니라 그의 첫 소설인「산골 나그네」를 잡지에 발

# Kim Yu-jeong

Kim Yu-jeong was born in the village of Sille in Chung-ri, Sindong-myeon, Chuncheon, Gangwon-do on February 12, 1908. He was the youngest child of Kim Chun-shik and Ms. Sim. His father was a wealthy landlord who owned most of the land in the village. The family moved to Seoul when Yu-jeong was six years old. While his father lived, Yu-jeong led an affluent life and was also showered with his family's affection. But the family's fortune began to decline after both his parents died when he was only a young child. Because his older brother squandered their inheritance, Yu-jeong spent much of his life in poverty. The large difference in their ages made him easy prey for his brother, who inflicted violence on him and their sisters. This childhood trauma left his spirit scarred, and inspired his story "Brother."

Upon graduating from Jaedong Elementary School, he entered Huimun High School in 1923, and there met a lifelong friend, An Hoe-nam, who went on to become a novelist. An advised him to write fiction,

표할 수 있도록 주선을 해주었고, 1935년《조선일보》
《조선중앙일보》신춘문예에서 김유정이 각각 당선작과
가작을 수상하는 데 큰 힘이 되었다. 그러나 학교생활
에 적응하지 못한 김유정은 결석을 하는 일이 잦았고
성적도 점점 나빠져 결국 낙제 끝에 5년 만에 졸업을 한
다.

　그 무렵 김유정은 다섯 살 연상인 기생 박녹주를 우
연히 만나 짝사랑에 빠진다. 상대방은 그에게 냉담했지
만 김유정은 대담하고도 열정적인 편지를 끊임없이 보
냈다 한다. 그의 사랑은 다소 광적인 면을 가지고 있었
는데, 이러한 경험은「두꺼비」「생의 반려」등의 소설에
반영되어 있다. 이들 소설에서는 어머니의 사랑을 받지
못한 주인공이 나이 많은 기생에게 집착하는 것으로 묘
사되는데, 김유정은 평생 사랑다운 사랑도 해보지 못했
고 그 주위에는 들병이 같은 매춘 여성들밖에 없었다.
이러한 애정 결핍은 등단 이후 잡지에서 본 여성 박봉
자에게도 박녹주와 같은 짝사랑의 감정을 느끼고 편지
공세를 했던 것에서도 알 수 있다.

　1930년에는 연희전문학교 문과에 입학하였으나 한
학기도 지나지 않아 제명당한다. 늑막염 진단을 받은

arranged for his first story, "Wanderer Among the Hills," to appear in a literary magazine, and helped him win short story contests sponsored by the *Chosun Ilbo* and the *Chosun Joongang Ilbo* in 1935. But Kim did not take well to school life and often skipped classes. It took him five years to graduate because of low grades.

Around this time, he met Park Nok-ju, a *kisaeng* (courtesan) who was five years his senior, and developed a crush on her. The female entertainer ignored him, but he kept sending her bold and passionate love letters. His infatuation was immortalized in his stories "Toad" and "Life's Companion." In them, the protagonists, deprived of their mother's affection, end up clinging to older courtesans. In fact, Kim never entered into a genuine love affair throughout his life, and instead sought the company of prostitutes. Starved for affection, he fell in love with Park Bong-ja, after seeing her picture in a magazine, and sent her sheaves of love letters, similar to his behavior to Park Nok-ju.

He enrolled in the department of literature at Yonhui College in 1930, only to be expelled after one semester. Diagnosed with pleurisy, he returned to his hometown, where he sought refuge in de-

것도 한 원인이 되어 낙망 끝에 형이 있는 춘천 실레마을에 가서 방랑 생활을 하며 들병이들과 친해진다. 한 해 뒤에는 다시 서울로 올라와 보성전문학교 상과에 입학하나 곧 자퇴하고 충청도 예산의 금광을 떠돌아다닌다. 이때의 경험은 「금 따는 콩밭」 「노다지」 같은 금광 열풍을 그린 소설에 반영되었다.

그러나 곧 금광 생활은 접고 실레마을로 돌아가 야학당(이후 금병의숙)을 열고 노인회, 부인회 등을 조직하는 등 농촌 계몽 활동을 벌인다. 약 2년 동안의 농촌 생활은 그에게 실로 커다란 경험이 되는데, 농촌의 하층 계급과 어울리며 그들의 언어, 생활 습관, 가난 등을 공유하였던 것이다. 그의 소설에 나타나는 풍부하고 정감 있는 향토적 언어 구사나 농민 생활의 현실성 있는 묘사, 민중들의 낙천적인 유머 등은 이때의 경험에서 비롯되었다. 처녀작 「심청」도 이 시기에 창작된 것이다.

1933년 서울로 올라온 그는 안회남의 도움으로 「산골나그네」 「총각과 맹꽁이」를 잡지에 게재하지만, 문단의 주목을 받지 못하고 게다가 나중에 사망 원인이 되는 폐결핵 판정을 받기까지 한다. 그러나 이러한 곤경은 오히려 그에게 창작 의지를 불태우는 동기가 되었기에

bauchery. The following year, he went to Seoul and joined the department of commerce at Boseong College, but dropped out before long to prospect for gold. He drew on this experience to portray the frenzy of the gold rush in "Plucking Gold in a Field of Beans" and "Bonanza." Before long, though, he also gave up this life and returned to his hometown to open a night school. He led a campaign to educate the people in the countryside by organizing associations of the elderly and women. Two years' immersion among the peasants helped him to learn their language and habits, and to understand the reality of poverty. The experience is manifested in his rich and earthy language, realistic portrayal of peasant life, and abundance of humor in his stories. "Simcheong" was written during this period.

Upon returning to Seoul in 1933, he published "Wanderer Among the Hills" and "Bachelor and Frogs" in a literary magazine with the help of An Hoe-nam, but it drew little attention from the literary community. He was also diagnosed with pulmonary tuberculosis, which would later claim his life. These hardships, however, motivated him in his writing. He wrote several stories during this period, including "Scoundrels," "Intimacy," and "Baby." He revised

그는「만부방」「정분」「애기」등 여러 편의 소설을 쓴다. 그 가운데「소낙비」와「노다지」를 고쳐 신춘문예에 응모하였고, 이 두 소설은 각기 《조선일보》 당선작, 《조선중앙일보》 가작으로 뽑혀 김유정은 화려하게 문단에 등장한다. 이후 2년 남짓한 시간은 그가 정열적이고 집중적으로 소설을 발표한 시기였다. 그의 대표작이라 할 수 있는「봄·봄」「동백꽃」등 20여 편의 소설이 이 시기에 발표된다. 이상, 박태원 등과 친교를 맺어 구인회에 가입하는 것도 이때였다.

그러는 사이 결핵은 점점 심해졌으나 가난에 시달려 치료도 제대로 할 수 없는 형편에 처하게 된 김유정을 위해 문단에서는 병고작가 구조 운동이 일어나기도 한다. 여러 곳을 전전하며 요양을 하던 김유정이 마지막에 이른 곳은 경기도 광주의 누이 집이었고 이곳에서도 그는 창작의 붓을 멈추지 않았다. 그러던 그는 1937년 3월 29일 사망하였다.

"Rain Shower" and "Bonanza" and entered them in contests organized by the *Chosun Ilbo* and the *Chosun Joonang Ilbo*, and was finally noticed by the literary community when he won both contests. For the next two years, he published about 20 stories, including representative works such as "Spring, Spring" and "Camellias." He became a member of Kuinhoe [the Society of Nine] after befriending Yi Sang and Pak Taewon.

In the meantime, his tuberculosis worsened, as poverty prevented him from seeking medical treatment, prompting the literary community to launch a campaign on his behalf. He moved from place to place to get a change of air, and ended up in his sister's house in Gwangju, Gyeonggi-do. He never stopped writing, even with his illness. He succumbed to pulmonary tuberculosis on March 29, 1937.

번역 **전승희** Translated by Jeon Seung-hee

서울대학교와 하버드대학교에서 영문학과 비교문학으로 박사 학위를 받았으며, 현재 하버드대학교 한국학 연구소의 연구원으로 재직하며 아시아 문예 계간지 《ASIA》 편집위원으로 활동 중이다. 현대 한국문학 및 세계문학을 다룬 논문을 다수 발표했으며, 바흐친의 『장편소설과 민중언어』, 제인 오스틴의 『오만과 편견』 등을 공역했다. 1988년 한국여성연구소의 창립과 《여성과 사회》의 창간에 참여했고, 2002년부터 보스턴 지역 피학대 여성을 위한 단체인 '트랜지션하우스' 운영에 참여해 왔다. 2006년 하버드대학교 한국학 연구소에서 '한국 현대사와 기억'을 주제로 한 워크숍을 주관했다.

Jeon Seung-hee is a member of the Editorial Board of *ASIA*, is a Fellow at the Korea Institute, Harvard University. She received a Ph.D. in English Literature from Seoul National University and a Ph.D. in Comparative Literature from Harvard University. She has presented and published numerous papers on modern Korean and world literature. She is also a co-translator of Mikhail Bakhtin's *Novel and the People's Culture* and Jane Austen's *Pride and Prejudice*. She is a founding member of the Korean Women's Studies Institute and of the biannual Women's Studies' journal *Women and Society* (1988), and she has been working at 'Transition House,' the first and oldest shelter for battered women in New England. She organized a workshop entitled "The Politics of Memory in Modern Korea" at the Korea Institute, Harvard University, in 2006. She also served as an advising committee member for the Asia-Africa Literature Festival in 2007 and for the POSCO Asian Literature Forum in 2008.

감수 **데이비드 윌리엄 홍** Edited by David William Hong

미국 일리노이주 시카고에서 태어났다. 일리노이대학교에서 영문학을, 뉴욕대학교에서 영어교육을 공부했다. 지난 2년간 서울에 거주하면서 처음으로 한국인과 아시아계 미국인 문학에 깊이 몰두할 기회를 가졌다. 현재 뉴욕에서 거주하며 강의와 저술 활동을 한다.

David William Hong was born in 1986 in Chicago, Illinois. He studied English Literature at the University of Illinois and English Education at New York University. For the past two years, he lived in Seoul, South Korea, where he was able to immerse himself in Korean and Asian-American literature for the first time. Currently, he lives in New York City, teaching and writing.

바이링궐 에디션 한국 대표 소설 096
# 봄·봄

2015년 1월 9일 초판 1쇄 발행

지은이 김유정 | 옮긴이 전승희 | 펴낸이 김재범
감수 데이비드 윌리엄 홍 | 기획위원 정은경, 전성태, 이경재
편집 정수인, 이은혜, 김형욱, 윤단비 | 관리 박신영
펴낸곳 (주)아시아 | 출판등록 2006년 1월 27일 제406-2006-000004호
주소 서울특별시 동작구 서달로 161-1(흑석동 100-16)
전화 02.821.5055 | 팩스 02.821.5057 | 홈페이지 www.bookasia.org
ISBN 979-11-5662-067-9 (set) | 979-11-5662-073-0 (04810)
값은 뒤표지에 있습니다.


Bi-lingual Edition Modern Korean Literature 096
# Spring, Spring

**Written by** Kim Yu-jeong I **Translated by** Jeon Seung-hee
**Published by** Asia Publishers I 161-1, Seodal-ro, Dongjak-gu, Seoul, Korea
**Homepage Address** www.bookasia.org I **Tel**. (822).821.5055 I **Fax**. (822).821.5057
First published in Korea by Asia Publishers 2015
ISBN 979-11-5662-067-9 (set) | 979-11-5662-073-0 (04810)

## 바이링궐 에디션 한국 대표 소설

한국문학의 가장 중요하고 첨예한 문제의식을 가진 작가들의 대표작을 주제별로 선정!
하버드 한국학 연구원 및 세계 각국의 한국문학 전문 번역진이 참여한 번역 시리즈!
미국 하버드대학교와 컬럼비아대학교 동아시아학과, 캐나다 브리티시컬럼비아대학교 아시아
학과 등 해외 대학에서 교재로 채택!

## 바이링궐 에디션 한국 대표 소설 set 1

### 분단 Division

01 병신과 머저리-**이청준** The Wounded-Yi Cheong-jun
02 어둠의 혼-**김원일** Soul of Darkness-Kim Won-il
03 순이삼촌-**현기영** Sun-i Samch'on-Hyun Ki-young
04 엄마의 말뚝 1-**박완서** Mother's Stake I-Park Wan-suh
05 유형의 땅-**조정래** The Land of the Banished-Jo Jung-rae

### 산업화 Industrialization

06 무진기행-**김승옥** Record of a Journey to Mujin-Kim Seung-ok
07 삼포 가는 길-**황석영** The Road to Sampo-Hwang Sok-yong
08 아홉 켤레의 구두로 남은 사내-**윤흥길** The Man Who Was Left as Nine Pairs
of Shoes-Yun Heung-gil
09 돌아온 우리의 친구-**신상웅** Our Friend's Homecoming-Shin Sang-ung
10 원미동 시인-**양귀자** The Poet of Wŏnmi-dong-Yang Kwi-ja

### 여성 Women

11 중국인 거리-**오정희** Chinatown-Oh Jung-hee
12 풍금이 있던 자리-**신경숙** The Place Where the Harmonium Was-Shin
Kyung-sook
13 하나코는 없다-**최윤** The Last of Hanak'o-Ch'oe Yun
14 인간에 대한 예의-**공지영** Human Decency-Gong Ji-young
15 빈처-**은희경** Poor Man's Wife-Eun Hee-kyung

## 바이링궐 에디션 한국 대표 소설 set 2

### 자유 Liberty

16 필론의 돼지-**이문열** Pilon's Pig-Yi Mun-yol
17 슬로우 불릿-**이대환** Slow Bullet-Lee Dae-hwan
18 직선과 독가스-**임철우** Straight Lines and Poison Gas-Lim Chul-woo
19 깃발-**홍희담** The Flag-Hong Hee-dam
20 새벽 출정-**방현석** Off to Battle at Dawn-Bang Hyeon-seok

**사랑과 연애 Love and Love Affairs**

21 별을 사랑하는 마음으로-**윤후명** With the Love for the Stars-Yun Hu-myong

22 목련공원-**이승우** Magnolia Park-Lee Seung-u

23 칼에 찔린 자국-**김인숙** Stab-Kim In-suk

24 회복하는 인간-**한강** Convalescence-Han Kang

25 트렁크-**정이현** In the Trunk-Jeong Yi-hyun

**남과 북 South and North**

26 판문점-**이호철** Panmunjom-Yi Ho-chol

27 수난 이대-**하근찬** The Suffering of Two Generations-Ha Geun-chan

28 분지-**남정현** Land of Excrement-Nam Jung-hyun

29 봄 실상사-**정도상** Spring at Silsangsa Temple-Jeong Do-sang

30 은행나무 사랑-**김하기** Gingko Love-Kim Ha-kee

**바이링궐 에디션 한국 대표 소설 set 3**

**서울 Seoul**

31 눈사람 속의 검은 항아리-**김소진** The Dark Jar within the Snowman-Kim So-jin

32 오후, 가로지르다-**하성란** Traversing Afternoon-Ha Seong-nan

33 나는 봉천동에 산다-**조경란** I Live in Bongcheon-dong-Jo Kyung-ran

34 그렇습니까? 기린입니다-**박민규** Is That So? I'm A Giraffe-Park Min-gyu

35 성탄특선-**김애란** Christmas Specials-Kim Ae-ran

**전통 Tradition**

36 무자년의 가을 사흘-**서정인** Three Days of Autumn, 1948-Su Jung-in

37 유자소전-**이문구** A Brief Biography of Yuja-Yi Mun-gu

38 향기로운 우물 이야기-**박범신** The Fragrant Well-Park Bum-shin

39 월행-**송기원** A Journey under the Moonlight-Song Ki-won

40 협죽도 그늘 아래-**성석제** In the Shade of the Oleander-Song Sok-ze

**아방가르드 Avant-garde**

41 아겔다마-**박상룡** Akeldama-Park Sang-ryoong

42 내 영혼의 우물-**최인석** A Well in My Soul-Choi In-seok

43 당신에 대해서-**이인성** On You-Yi In-seong

44 회색 時-**배수아** Time In Gray-Bae Su-ah

45 브라운 부인-**정영문** Mrs. Brown-Jung Young-moon

## 바이링궐 에디션 한국 대표 소설 set 4

### 디아스포라 Diaspora

46 속옷-김남일 Underwear-Kim Nam-il

47 상하이에 두고 온 사람들-공선옥 People I Left in Shanghai-Gong Sun-ok

48 모두에게 복된 새해-김연수 Happy New Year to Everyone-Kim Yeon-su

49 코끼리-김재영 The Elephant-Kim Jae-young

50 먼지별-이경 Dust Star-Lee Kyung

### 가족 Family

51 혜자의 눈꽃-천승세 Hye-ja's Snow-Flowers-Chun Seung-sei

52 아베의 가족-전상국 Ahbe's Family-Jeon Sang-guk

53 문 앞에서-이동하 Outside the Door-Lee Dong-ha

54 그리고, 축제-이혜경 And Then the Festival-Lee Hye-kyung

55 봄밤-권여선 Spring Night-Kwon Yeo-sun

### 유머 Humor

56 오늘의 운세-한창훈 Today's Fortune-Han Chang-hoon

57 새-전성태 Bird-Jeon Sung-tae

58 밀수록 다시 가까워지는-이기호 So Far, and Yet So Near-Lee Ki-ho

59 유리방패-김중혁 The Glass Shield-Kim Jung-hyuk

60 전당포를 찾아서-김종광 The Pawnshop Chase-Kim Chong-kwang

## 바이링궐 에디션 한국 대표 소설 set 5

### 관계 Relationship

61 도둑견습 – 김주영 Robbery Training-Kim Joo-young

62 사랑하라, 희망 없이 – 윤영수 Love, Hopelessly-Yun Young-su

63 봄날 오후, 과부 셋 – 정지아 Spring Afternoon, Three Widows-Jeong Ji-a

64 유턴 지점에 보물지도를 묻다 – 윤성희 Burying a Treasure Map at the U-turn-Yoon Sung-hee

65 쁘이거나 쓰이거나 – 백가흠 Puy, Thuy, Whatever-Paik Ga-huim

### 일상의 발견 Discovering Everyday Life

66 나는 음식이다 – 오수연 I Am Food-Oh Soo-yeon

67 트럭 – 강영숙 Truck-Kang Young-sook

68 통조림 공장 – 편혜영 The Canning Factory-Pyun Hye-young

69 꽃 – 부희령 Flowers-Pu Hee-ryoung

70 피의일요일 – 윤이형 BloodySunday-Yun I-hyeong

### 금기와 욕망 Taboo and Desire

71 북소리 - 송영 Drumbeat-Song Yong
72 발칸의 장미를 내게 주었네 - 정미경 He Gave Me Roses of the Balkans-Jung Mi-kyung
73 아무도 돌아오지 않는 밤 - 김숨 The Night Nobody Returns Home-Kim Soom
74 젓가락여자 - 천운영 Chopstick Woman-Cheon Un-yeong
75 아직 일어나지 않은 일 - 김미월 What Has Yet to Happen-Kim Mi-wol

### 바이링궐 에디션 한국 대표 소설 set 6

### 운명 Fate

76 언니를 놓치다 - 이경자 Losing a Sister-Lee Kyung-ja
77 아들 - 윤정모 Father and Son-Yoon Jung-mo
78 명두 - 구효서 Relics-Ku Hyo-seo
79 모독 - 조세희 Insult-Cho Se-hui
80 화요일의 강 - 손홍규 Tuesday River-Son Hong-gyu

### 미의 사제들 Aesthetic Priests

81 고수 - 이외수 Grand Master-Lee Oisoo
82 말을 찾아서 - 이순원 Looking for a Horse-Lee Soon-won
83 상춘곡 - 윤대녕 Song of Everlasting Spring-Youn Dae-nyeong
84 삭매와 자미 - 김별아 Sakmae and Jami-Kim Byeol-ah
85 저만치 혼자서 - 김훈 Alone Over There-Kim Hoon

### 식민지의 벌거벗은 자들 The Naked in the Colony

86 감자 - 김동인 Potatoes-Kim Tong-in
87 운수 좋은 날 - 현진건 A Lucky Day-Hyŏn Chin'gŏn
88 탈출기 - 최서해 Escape-Ch'oe So-hae
89 과도기 - 한설야 Transition-Han Seol-ya
90 지하촌 - 강경애 The Underground Village-Kang Kyŏng-ae